For Josie and Oliver

First U.S. paperback edition 2012

Library of Congress Cataloging-in-Publication Data is available.
Library of Congress Catalog Card Number 9447190

ISBN 978-0-7636-2042-4 (board book)
ISBN 978-0-7636-6124-3 (paperback)

12 13 14 15 16 17 SCP 10 9 8 7 6 5 4 3 2 1

Printed in Humen, Dongguan, China

This book was typeset in Lucy Cousins.
The illustrations were done in gouache.

Candlewick Press
99 Dover Street
Somerville, Massachusetts 02144

visit us at www.candlewick.com

CANDLEWICK PRESS

Za-Za's
Baby Brother

Lucy Cousins

My mom is going to have a baby.

She has a big fat tummy. There's not much room for a hug.

Dad took Mom to the hospital.

When the baby was born
we went to see Mom.

When Mom came home
she was very tired.
I had to be very quiet
and help Dad
take care of her.

What a good boy!

Ooh, he's gorgeous.

I played by myself.

Dad was always busy.

Mom was always busy.

"Dad, will you read me a story?"
"Not now, Za-Za. We're going shopping soon."

So I hugged the baby...

and I pushed him...

and I built him a tower.

He was nice.
It was fun.

When the baby got tired Mom put him to bed.

Then I got my
hug...

and a bedtime story.